The Scam of
the Screwball
Wizards

Bethany House Books by
Bill Myers

Bloodhounds, Inc.
CHILDREN'S MYSTERY SERIES

The Ghost of KRZY
The Mystery of the Invisible Knight
Phantom of the Haunted Church
Invasion of the UFOs
Fangs for the Memories
The Case of the Missing Minds
The Secret of the Ghostly Hot Rod
I Want My Mummy
The Curse of the Horrible Hair Day
The Scam of the Screwball Wizards

Nonfiction

The Dark Side of the Supernatural
Hot Topics, Tough Questions

Bill Myers' Web site: www.BillMyers.com

10
BloodHounds, INC.

The Scam of the Screwball Wizards

Bill Myers

with DAVE WIMBISH

BETHANY HOUSE PUBLISHERS
MINNEAPOLIS, MINNESOTA 55438

The Scam of the Screwball Wizards
Copyright © 2001
Bill Myers

Cover design by Lookout Design Group, Inc.

Published by Bethany House Publishers
A Ministry of Bethany Fellowship International
11400 Hampshire Avenue South
Bloomington, Minnesota 55438
www.bethanyhouse.com

Printed in the United States of America by
Bethany Press International, Bloomington, Minnesota 55438

Library of Congress Cataloging-in-Publication Data

Myers, Bill, 1953-
    The scam of the screwball wizards / by Bill Myers.
        p.   cm. — (Bloodhounds, Inc. ; 10)
Summary: When their friend Bear gets involved with a group of school misfits who model themselves after a popular fantasy book series, Sean and Melissa go undercover to reveal the truth about their "magical powers."
    ISBN 0-7642-2438-7 (pbk.)
    [1. Brothers and sisters—Fiction. 2. Schools—Fiction. 3. Mystery and detective stories. 4. Christian life—Fiction.] I. Title.
    PZ7.M98234 Sb   2001
    [Fic]—dc21   2001002565

For Stephen Bly:

A great writer who loves God.

BILL MYERS is a youth worker, creative writer, and film director who co-created the "McGee and Me!" book and video series; his work has received over forty national and international awards. His many books include THE INCREDIBLE WORLDS OF WALLY MCDOOGLE series; his teen books: *Hot Topics, Tough Questions; Faith Encounter;* and *Forbidden Doors;* as well as his adult novels: *When the Last Leaf Falls; Eli;* and the trilogy *Blood of Heaven, Threshold,* and *Fire of Heaven.*

Contents

Finally, brothers,
whatever is true, whatever is noble,
whatever is right, whatever is pure,
whatever is lovely, whatever is admirable—
if anything is excellent or praiseworthy—
think about such things.

Philippians 4:8

The Case Begins

SATURDAY, 16:42 PDST

"YEEOOWW!" Sean cried. "Get it off! Get it off!"

He staggered back and forth across Doc's laboratory, trying with all of his might to pull the huge, um . . . er . . . well, whatever it was . . . away from his ear.

"Good grief!" Melissa shouted. "What have you done now?" At first she couldn't tell what was trying to swallow her brother's face. Was it a snake? An elephant's trunk? Some sort of alien?

CLANK! CLANK! CLANK!

She spun around to see that it was connected to a miniature army tank. No, wait, it wasn't a tank. It was a giant, superpowerful vacuum cleaner. And the snake, or whatever it was, was actually the vacuum cleaner's hose. A hose that, at the moment, was doing its best to suck off Sean's left ear.

"GET IT OFF! GET IT OFF!"

Melissa grabbed the hose and yanked hard. It wouldn't budge. It was stuck to her brother's ear like Super Glue.

"Woof! Woof!" Slobs, the kids' huge bloodhound, danced around the room, barking in excitement as Sean, always a little dramatic, cried, "MY EAR! MY EAR! IT'S RIPPING MY EAR OFF!"

"Hold still!" Melissa shouted. "I can't get a good grip on this thing with you wiggling around like that! And it's not tearing your ear off. It's just kind of . . . turning it purple!"

Melissa strained with all her might, trying to pull the vacuum hose off Sean's ear. But it still wouldn't give an inch. She looked in Doc's direction, hoping that their inventor friend had seen Sean's problem.

She hadn't.

Instead, she was bent over her workbench, studying a complicated diagram. She was completely unaware of the struggle directly behind her. Being deaf, she hadn't heard a thing.

But that didn't stop Sean from yelling . . . or the vacuum cleaner from

*ROOOAAAAARRRR*ing.

"Slobs!" Melissa shouted. "Grab Doc! Get Doc's attention!"

Slobs stopped barking and cocked her head to one side.

"Doc!" Melissa pointed. "Get Doc!"

"Woof!" Immediately Slobs turned and ran toward Doc. Well, actually, she ran past Doc. To be more precise, she ran past Doc, out the door, and down the street toward their house. (Apparently, "Get Doc!" sounded an awful lot like "Go home, gobble up as much dinner as possible, then take a nice long nap!") Good ol' Slobs.

Meanwhile, Doc, who had been leaning over the counter for a long time, stood up, put her hands behind her head, and stretched. That's when her eyes caught the reflection from the mirror on the wall . . . and that's when her mouth dropped open. Because now, finally, she could see the fight that had been going on.

She grabbed a small black box off her workbench and whirled around to face Sean and Melissa. By now the two were flopping helplessly on the floor—like a couple of fish out of water. Actually, like a couple of fish that were about to be sucked up by one very powerful vacuum cleaner.

11

SATURDAY, 16:45 PDST

At this exact moment, across town, Spalding and KC sat on KC's front porch. The two weren't exactly Sean and Melissa's friends, but they weren't exactly their enemies, either. Both were holding their heads in their hands and sitting in thought.

It was strange how Spalding and KC could be such close buddies. They weren't anything alike. Spalding was the richest kid in Midvale and definitely the snobbiest. And KC was the toughest kid in Midvale, even though she was a girl.

Normally, wherever you saw the two of them together, you also saw Bear. He was their big, good-natured, slow-witted friend—a boy whose three favorite hobbies were eating, sleeping, and . . . well, eating.

But today he was nowhere to be seen.

After a long pause, KC finally spoke. "Well, I guess you're right," her gravelly little voice croaked. "I hate to do it, but I don't see any other way."

"Neither do I," Spalding said. "And no matter how annoying they might be, you must admit that they have solved a plethora of cases."

"Plethor-what?" KC asked.

"It means a lot," Spalding sighed. "Bloodhounds, Incorporated, has solved a lot of cases."

"I know," KC sighed in return. "I'll just keep reminding myself that what we're about to do is for Bear." She stood up. "Well, come on," she croaked. "Let's get going."

At the same time, on the outskirts of town, three boys slowly made their way down the steep stairs to the basement of the old Midvale Community Theater. The theater had moved to a newer, bigger location long ago, and the old building had stood lonely and abandoned ever since.

Well, almost abandoned.

One of the boys wore a blindfold. He was a chubby kid with hair that looked like it hadn't been washed in a week or combed in two. And if you're guessing it was Bear, you're guessing right.

The second kid led Bear along by his elbow to make sure he didn't fall. And the third boy—a tall redheaded guy—walked in front of them. He carried a flashlight in one hand and was shooting a can of Silly String onto the steps before them with the other.

SSSSsssss . . . SSSSsssss . . .

Bear hesitated a moment. "What's . . . what's that noise?" he asked.

"It's magic!" whispered the red-haired kid. "Pure, powerful magic."

When they reached the bottom of the stairs, they arrived at an old door. The boy with the flashlight gave a secret knock . . . and it slowly creaked open.

They stepped inside, then started down another shorter flight of wooden stairs.

SSSSsssss . . . SSSSsssss . . .

They reached the bottom of the steps. The room was cool and dark, lit only by a few candles. Faint whispers could be heard. There were people here, but who or how many, it was impossible to say.

"How long do I have to wear this blindfold?" Bear complained.

"Not much longer," another voice spoke from the darkness. "Are you certain you are willing to take the oath?"

Bear nervously cleared his throat. "Yes," he said.

"Are you ready to give your life?"

After the slightest pause and a little swallow, Bear gave his answer. "Yes . . ."

SATURDAY, 16:54 PDST

Back in Doc's lab, the inventor pushed furiously at the buttons of the control box in her hand. The big hose lurched once . . . twice . . . then finally let go of Sean's ear as it whined down and came to a stop.

Sean and his sister untangled themselves and struggled to their feet.

"My ear . . . is it . . . gone?" Sean asked as he reached for his aching ear.

"Don't worry," Melissa said, "I'm sure we can get you a plastic one."

"Plastic?" Sean cried. "I don't want . . ." At last he touched it. "Hey! It's still here. It's not torn off!"

"Of course not," Melissa laughed. "You have the same little pointy ear you've always had."

Sean gave her a look.

"How did you get that thing stuck to your face, anyway?" Melissa asked.

Sean shrugged. "I was just fooling around, and the next thing I knew, it was trying to rip my ear off." He turned toward Doc and signed the question: *What is this thing, anyway?*

Doc looked puzzled. *What do you mean, what is it?* she signed back.

Sean continued. *I mean . . . is it some kind of*

secret weapon? *Something Bloodhounds, Inc., can use to catch criminals?*

Doc smiled and stepped to one of the computer keyboards she kept close at hand.

What does it look like? she typed.

It looks like a vacuum cleaner, Melissa signed.

Doc's fingers flew over the keys. *Exactly. It's a vacuum cleaner.*

"It's her latest invention," said a high-pitched electronic voice from inside Sean's watch. "She calls it SuperVac. You know what they say . . . 'Cleanliness is the next best thing to being there.' "

Sean glanced down to his digital wristwatch. A tiny leprechaun-like creature with green skin and bright red hair smiled up at him. The little fellow glowed and pulsated with electric energy.

"Actually," Sean said, "the saying is, 'Cleanliness is next to godliness.' "

"Whatever," Jeremiah shrugged.

Jeremiah was one of Doc's first inventions, and her best. He really wasn't a person . . . but he sure came close. He spent most of his time hanging out in Sean's digital watch, or in Doc's lab computer. But he was also able to go just about anywhere there was electricity.

SuperVac is more than just some ordinary vacuum cleaner, Doc typed.

Still rubbing his ear, Sean whined, "You can say that again!"

Doc nodded and typed, *It uses a bipolar inversion of the electromagnetic field, coupled with oxidizer injectors to increase the subsonic flow.*

Melissa gently tapped Doc on the shoulder. *I'm sorry*, she signed, *but is there a chance of explaining that in English?*

Sure, she typed. *The SuperVac has one thousand times the suction power of a normal vacuum cleaner. Not only that, but it's completely self-propelled. When I get all the bugs worked out, it will be able to vacuum an entire house in just a few minutes—with minimal human involvement.*

Really? Melissa asked.

Just set the controls and let her go! With those tank treads, she can travel anywhere.

"Wow!" Sean said, walking over for a closer look at the machine. Sean's curiosity (which was a lot stronger than his common sense) was getting the better of him. *How fast can it go?* he asked.

Before Doc could answer, Sean snatched the controls out of her hands.

"Sean!" Melissa shouted. "Be careful!"

"Of course I'll be careful," he said. "What do you think I am, stupid or some—"

RRRRRRRRRR!

The SuperVac roared to life and . . .

roll, roll, roll

. . . raced around the room as Sean, Melissa, and Doc scrambled to get out of its way.

"Sean!" Melissa shrieked.

"I didn't mean to!" he cried.

The big machine circled the room once, twice, three times as its hose flipped and flopped in every direction until . . .

SHOOOP!

. . . it swallowed a stack of Doc's important papers. Then . . .

KA-CHINK!

. . . there went a bunch of her tools. And . . .

THWACK!

. . . say good-bye to the throw rug.

Picking up speed, the SuperVac bounced down the stairs and barged through the front door, where it headed out into the unsuspecting neighborhood.

Sean and Melissa ran after it as fast as they could,

shouting for the machine to stop as Sean frantically pushed the remote-control button over and over again. But nothing seemed to work. Instead, SuperVac actually seemed to be picking up speed. Soon it . . .

SHOOOOOOP!

. . . gobbled up the For Sale sign in the Simpsons' front yard. Then it . . .

SHOOP . . . SHOOP . . . SHOOP . . .

. . . cut a path through Mrs. McClellan's prize begonias. And finally . . .

ROARRRRRR!

OH NO! Could that possibly be Mrs. Tubbs out for an afternoon stroll with her huge and obnoxious cat, Precious?

Do you even have to ask?

And Doc's self-propelled vacuum cleaner was heading straight toward them.

"Run, Mrs. Tubbs!" Sean yelled. "Run!"

Unfortunately, Mrs. Tubbs didn't run. Instead, she stopped and just stood there.

"Do something!" Melissa shouted to her brother.

"Like what?"

"Anything!"

The SuperVac was closing in fast on Mrs. Tubbs and Precious.

"You know she's going to blame us for this," Melissa yelled. "She blames us for everything!"

"Well, who could blame her?!" Sean shouted back.

Although Mrs. Tubbs was not moving, Precious had other ideas. In a flash, the tremendously fat animal turned and ran. And Mrs. Tubbs, who still held the cat's leash, did a perfect

KER-WHACK!

belly flop onto the sidewalk. (Don't worry, she wasn't hurt. The woman is very well padded.)

"Precious, stop!" she screamed. "Stop!"

But he didn't stop. Instead, he ran right through Mrs. Oliver's prize rosebushes . . .

"OUCH!"

. . . straight through the Ortega family's cactus garden . . .

"OUCH! OUCH!"

. . . and out into the middle of the street, with Mrs. Tubbs banging and bouncing behind him every inch of the way. And behind her, the killer SuperVac continued to gain ground.

Then, at the last second, Precious zigged when he should have zagged and . . .

"MEOWWRRR . . . HISSS—" *SHOOOOOP!*

. . . he disappeared up the vacuum cleaner's hose.

Yes, as sad as it may be, poor Precious was now . . . *hiss*story.

2

Well, I'll Be
Phangdoodled

SATURDAY, 16:59 PDST

"My cat! My cat!"

Mrs. Tubbs was bruised and battered. Her wig sat
sideways on her head. But none of that mattered.
Instead, she shook her fist in anger as she ran toward
the vacuum cleaner. "You give me my cat back! You
give me my cat back!"

Finally SuperVac lumbered to a stop. It hiccuped a
couple of times . . . shot a spray of cat hair into the
air . . . and then suddenly shut down. The killer
machine had gobbled down tools, papers, a For Sale
sign, seventeen bushes, and at least three welcome
mats without a problem. But apparently, Precious was
more than it could handle.

Sean reached the lifeless SuperVac first. He

grabbed the hose and put it to his ear.

"Sean," Melissa shouted, "what are you doing? Don't you remember the last time you—"

"I hear something!" he said. "Listen!" He held the hose to his sister's ear.

"mew . . ."

A tiny, kittenlike voice came from the other end. It sounded so weak and pathetic.

"It's Precious!" Melissa shouted. "He's alive!"

"But how do we get him out?" Sean asked.

"There must be some way to get in there," Melissa answered. "Look!" she pointed down to the machine. "Maybe if we took off that control panel!"

Sean nodded and stooped down to fumble with a series of buttons and levers. But nothing happened.

"I don't know," he said, "I can't seem to—"

WHAPPP!

Melissa gave SuperVac a good swift kick and instantly . . .

KER-THUNK!

. . . the side panel fell off.

Sean reached his hand into the guts of the machine, rummaged around for a while, and finally pulled out one dusty, wide-eyed, and *completely bald* cat. Other than that, Precious was fine. Except for trembling with fear and looking very much like a miniature pink pig, he was just fine.

But Mrs. Tubbs didn't seem to notice. "Oh, my Precious," she cooed, "come to mama."

The huge cat leaped in his owner's direction. Unfortunately, Mrs. Tubbs had forgotten just how big he was until . . .

"OOOOOF!"

. . . Precious hit her squarely in the chest, and they both fell to the ground in a cloud of dust.

Mrs. Tubbs quickly leaped up, not even noticing that her wig was now on backward. "I've had enough!" she growled. "You will be hearing from my attorney!"

"But, Mrs. Tubbs," Melissa protested in her sweetest voice, "we didn't mean to—"

"Come on, Precious!" Mrs. Tubbs interrupted. "Let's go home."

They both stuck their noses high into the air, turned, and began waddling away. Their attempts to look dignified might have worked a bit better . . . if the seat wasn't completely torn out of Mrs. Tubbs' pants . . . if her blouse wasn't shredded . . . and if her wig wasn't on backward. As for Precious, he no longer looked like a pampered blue-blood. Instead, he had the appearance of an old alley cat who had fought an electric shaver . . . and lost.

Sean and Melissa held off laughing as long as they could, but as soon as Mrs. Tubbs and Precious were out of earshot, they doubled over.

"You know . . . ho-ho, hee-hee . . . we really shouldn't be laughing about this," Melissa gasped between laughter.

"You're . . . ha-ha . . . absolutely . . . hee-hee . . . right!" Sean laughed. "She's . . . hee-hee . . . going to get us in all kinds of . . . ho-ho . . . trouble!"

But their laughter was short-lived.

Suddenly a voice demanded, "What's so funny?"

Melissa turned around to see KC and Spalding arriving on their bicycles. "Oh, hi, guys," she said. "Nothing's funny, really. I mean, not when you stop to think about it."

"Where's Bear?" Sean asked.

"That's an excellent question," Spalding answered. "Precisely the reason we wish to converse with you."

"Yeah," KC agreed. "We've been looking all over for you guys." Then, pointing at SuperVac, she asked, "What is that thing, anyway?"

"A vacuum cleaner," Sean answered.

"Vacuum cleaner!" KC exclaimed. "What's it doing

way out here? Were you vacuuming the street?"

"Of course," Melissa shrugged. "You can never be too neat, you know."

Spalding turned in a circle, looking at the destruction all around him. "It appears to me that you may wish to try again," he said.

"Maybe," Sean agreed. Then, quickly changing the subject, he asked, "Now, what were you saying about Bear?"

The four kids started down Oak Street. As KC and Spalding walked alongside their bikes, they told their story.

"Something has happened to Bear," KC said.

"Like what?" Sean asked. "Is he hurt?"

"No."

"Is he missing?"

"No."

"Did he get robbed?"

"No, it's nothing like that." KC shook her head. "It's more like . . . like—"

Spalding interrupted, "If you ask me, it's as if he is having some type of psychotic episode."

"Psycho-whoozit?" Sean asked.

Spalding sighed. "He is acting crazy."

"Crazy?" Melissa said. "How so?"

"Well . . ." Spalding stood still and thought for a

moment. "It is fairly difficult to pinpoint. But as an example, he does not want anything to do with either KC or me."

Melissa caught her brother's eye, and they both knew what the other was thinking: *Wanting to avoid these two is ANYTHING but crazy.*

"He also gets angry a lot," KC added.

Now that *was* something strange. Bear never got angry about anything . . . ever.

"And the other day, we asked him to go with us to the Pizza Barn—"

"Our treat," Spalding interjected.

"—and he turned us down," KC said.

"He what?!" Sean practically shouted.

"He turned down pizza," KC repeated.

"This *is* serious!" Melissa said. (Bear refusing food was worth a story on the local news, and when the day came that Bear turned down pizza . . . well, you'd better call in the people from *The X-Files*.)

"So what do you want us to do?" Sean asked.

"We want to engage your services," Spalding replied.

"Engage our. . . ?"

"We want to hire you," KC explained.

Spalding nodded. "We'll pay Bloodhounds, Incorporated, $100 to find out what's going on with

Bear. That's nearly half my allowance for an entire week."

"All right!" Sean beamed. "You've got yourself a deal."

SATURDAY, 17:51 PDST

Less than an hour later, Sean and Melissa were walking up the sidewalk to Bear's front door.

"This is going to be a piece of cake," Sean whispered to his sister. "We'll go in, spend a few minutes talking to Bear, he'll tell us what's wrong, and then we'll go collect our hundred bucks."

"I hope you're right," she answered. "But if you ask me, this is a strange job for Bloodhounds, Incorporated. I mean, nobody's committed a crime or anything."

Sean shrugged and pushed the doorbell.

DING-DONG!

"A hundred bucks is a hundred bucks," he said.

They waited, but nobody came to the door.

After several moments, Melissa offered, "Maybe nobody's home."

Sean put his ear to the door. "No, I hear someone moving around in there."

He jabbed at the doorbell again.

DING-DONG! DING-DONG!

More waiting. Then, finally, they heard the sound of footsteps approaching from inside. The door opened just a sliver, and an eye peeked out.

"Yeah?" someone said.

"Is that you, Bear?" Sean asked.

"Whadd'ya want?" Bear replied coldly.

"We just thought we'd stop by for a few minutes," Sean said. "We haven't seen you around for a while and we . . . uh . . ."

"We miss you," Melissa finished her brother's sentence. She gave Bear her sweetest smile. "Aren't you going to invite us in?"

"I'm kinda busy."

"We won't stay long," Melissa promised. "And we really *have* missed you."

After a moment's hesitation, Bear slowly pulled open the door. "Okay, come in—but I don't got much time." In his other hand, Bear held a book with a strange title: *Cecil Shoemaker and the Magic Phangdoodle.*

Sean and Melissa exchanged surprised looks. They

had never known Bear to read anything before (unless it was to find out how many Twinkies came in a package).

Suddenly Bear's beagle, Brandi, trotted across the room with her supper dish in her mouth.

Bear sighed. "Guess I forgot to feed ya again," he said. He turned and gestured down the hallway. "If you guys want, you can go on back to my room while I feed the dog. I'll be there in a minute."

Sean and Melissa agreed and headed down the hall. Once inside the bedroom, Sean pushed aside a pile of dirty clothes and sat on Bear's bed. "Have a seat," he said.

Melissa looked at the assortment of underwear, crumpled papers, and candy-bar wrappers that covered the bed. "Uh, no thanks," she said. "I think it's safer if I just stand." Then, after a moment, she continued. "I can't imagine Bear being interested in a book. I wonder what it's about."

Sean shrugged. "Well, at least he's reading, so that's good."

Melissa shook her head. "I'm not so sure . . ." She glanced over at Bear's desk. "What's this?" she waded through the debris and picked up a strange-looking trading card. On its front was a cartoonlike creature with the name *Phangmeister* written under it.

Sean took the card from her and flipped it over. He began to read: "Card number thirty-four in the series: *Cecil Shoemaker and the Magic Phangdoodle*."

"That's the name of the book he was reading," Melissa said.

Sean continued reading. "The Phangmeister is an expert in the art of black magic. With his power, you can cast spells and—"

Suddenly Bear was in the room and snatching the card out of Sean's hands. "Hey, I wondered where that went," he said. "Thanks for finding it!" Then, without another word, he quickly stuffed the card in his pants pocket.

"Is that part of a new game or something?" Sean asked.

"Nah, it ain't nothing," Bear said. But the way his eyes kept shifting and glancing around, it was obvious he wasn't telling the whole truth.

"Can I see it?" Melissa asked.

"I said it's nothing," Bear snapped. He looked at his watch. "You know what? I just realized I'm late for my . . . er . . . ah . . . my ice-skating class."

"Your—" Melissa almost choked on the words— "ice-skating class?"

"Yeah, what's wrong with that?"

"Nothing," Sean smiled. "Nothing at all."

"Hate to be rude, but I got no time to visit," Bear said. "Gotta practice the old triple axel, you know." As if proving his point, Bear whirled around three times. He might have appeared more graceful if he hadn't . . .

KE-RASHed

. . . into his dresser and . . .

KE-THUDed

. . . backward onto the floor. But he quickly jumped up. "Like I said, I need some practice. You guys gotta go . . . now!"

Sean and Melissa nodded, and he quickly ushered them out of the house. Once they were safely outside, Melissa turned to her brother. "What in the world was that all about? He couldn't get rid of us fast enough."

"I don't know," Sean answered. "But I know one thing. Spalding and KC were right. Something is majorly wrong with Bear."

SATURDAY, 18:45 PDST

As they headed toward their house, Sean kept glancing at his watch. Melissa could tell he was deep in thought and in a hurry to get home. In fact, he kept walking faster and faster until Melissa nearly had to run to keep up with him.

By the time they got to their front door, he yanked it open and ran up the stairs. Melissa stayed right behind. "What are you thinking?" she huffed. "You got a (*gasp, gasp*) good idea?"

"I sure do!" he exclaimed as he ran into his room, clicked on the TV, and flopped onto his bed.

Melissa slowed to a stop. "Your great idea is to watch TV?" she demanded.

"You bet," he answered. "Tonight is the big finale of *Who Wants to Be a Gazillionaire?*"

"But, Sean, we've gotta find out—"

"Ssshhh!" He frowned. "I just want to find out if he gets the last questions right and—oh no!" Sean pointed angrily at the TV set. "What's he doing on there?"

It was Rafael Ruelas, no doubt giving another late-breaking news report.

"Great!" Sean complained. "Just great. It's another one of his stupid reports. I wonder what's going on this time. Maybe somebody's cat is stuck in a tree."

Sean's sarcasm was well-founded. Rafael Ruelas had become known around Midvale as "The reporter who cried wolf." His special reports were never about anything special—just a way to get on television. He figured sooner or later the popular news show *Good Morning United States* would call and offer him a multimillion-dollar job. In the meantime, the citizens of Midvale would just have to get used to seeing his face . . . as often as he could get himself on TV.

"This is Rafael Ruelas, coming to you from the Midvale Toy Emporium," he said. "There's excitement in the air here because this store has just received a huge shipment of the latest craze to capture the attention of America's youth. And that, of course, would be Cecil Shoemaker and all the wonderful, mystical creatures of the Magic Phangdoodle."

A close-up of one of the cards appeared on the screen.

"Look!" Melissa shouted. "That's the same card Bear had!"

The camera cut back to Rafael Ruelas, interviewing the store's owner. "So tell us about these Phangdoodle cards," Ruelas asked.

"Oh, they're great," the man replied. "They're fun and educational. Teachers love them, and parents don't have to worry about them because they're completely harmless."

Behind them, people began pushing and shoving one another, trying to get at the cards.

"You say these cards and books are completely harmless?" Ruelas asked.

A woman behind them suddenly punched a man in the nose.

"OW!"

"Completely," the owner insisted.

"I'll teach you to hit me!" the man behind them shouted.

The store owner raised his voice, trying to drown out the commotion. "Actually, they're better than harmless," he said. "They're getting kids all across our nation to start reading."

As he spoke, a full-fledged brawl broke out behind him. And a moment later, police with billy clubs were rushing in to break it up. But of course, Rafael Ruelas was too impressed with himself to notice.

"So there you have it, folks," he said, doing his best to sound charming and full of authority. "Something your kids are going to love. Something that just might change their lives. And it's all here at the Midvale Toy Emporium!" He grinned broadly as punches, kicks, slaps, and shouting were going on in the background. Lots and lots of shouting . . .

3

An UnBEARable Bear

MONDAY, 7:05 PDST

The door to Sean's bedroom flew open with such force that it . . .

BAMMed!

. . . against the wall.

"What . . . who. . . ?" Sean jerked up and tried to rub the sleep out of his eyes. In the early-morning light, he could just barely make out his father standing beside a very strange and unfamiliar woman. Who was she?

"Good news, son!" His dad grinned broadly. "Aunt Grizelda has decided to move in with us. Isn't that terrific?!"

"Uh . . . I . . . er . . . " Sean struggled for the right words to say. Aunt Grizelda was his dad's oldest sister, and Sean had always considered her proof that every family tree has a few nuts.

Now it was Aunt Grizelda's turn to grin. "We've talked it over and I'm going to do all the cooking from now on!" she said.

"And you know what that means!" Dad beamed. "Turnips with every meal!"

"That's right," Aunt Grizelda said as she started counting on her fingers. "Fried turnips, mashed turnips, grilled turnips, creamed turnips, turnips and chocolate sauce, turnips and mustard . . ."

"And for dessert?" Dad asked, licking his lips.

"Turnip-upside-down cake!" she cried, clapping her hands.

"My favorite!" Dad also clapped.

Sean would have joined in the applause, except it's kinda hard to clap in excitement when your stomach is flip-flopping in sheer terror.

"And you know what else, son?" Dad asked.

"I'm not sure I want to," Sean mumbled.

Dad turned to the woman. "Go ahead! Show him!"

Suddenly Aunt Grizelda held out a pair of bunny pajamas (complete with little feet and a cotton bunny tail). "You're going to look so adorable in these!" she squealed. She ran to Sean and threw her arms around him. "Oh, I just want to hug and kiss you to pieces!"

And that's exactly what she did. Before he could

stop her, she began kissing him on the cheek again and again until . . .

"Gag! Ugh!"

. . . she started to lick him all over the face!

"AUGH!" He tried pushing her away, but she wouldn't budge. And her breath? It was terrible. Smelled like . . . like dog food! "What are you doing?" he shouted.

"She's trying to wake you up!" his father said, only he sounded exactly like Melissa. Wait a second! Suddenly Aunt Grizelda had turned into some kind of animal! A dog! A *huge* dog! A huge dog that looked a lot like Slobs! And the reason was simple.

She *was* Slobs!

Suddenly it was Slobs who was standing over him, licking his face.

And more suddenly still, a wave of relief washed over Sean. "Boy, am I glad to see you!" he gasped between licks. Slobs increased her licking speed until Sean had to push her away. "Stop it, girl! You're drooling all over me. Stop it, now. Stop it."

Finally, reluctantly, Slobs jumped off Sean's bed.

"You better get up," Melissa said. She was standing in the doorway to his room. "It's getting late."

"It is?" Sean picked up the clock on his nightstand. "Yikes!" He couldn't be late to school again or he'd be in detention for a week.

"By the way, what were you dreaming about?" Melissa asked.

"Dreaming?"

"You kept screaming something about turnips."

"Oh yeah," Sean said, a smile creeping around his lips. It was just a dream. Thank goodness it was only a dream.

MONDAY, 10:14 PDST

"And so, in order to find the square root of—" Suddenly Mr. Spencer turned from the chalkboard and stared at Bear, who was whispering loudly to the boy in front of him.

"Mr. Thompson," Mr. Spencer said, pushing his glasses up on his nose. "Is there something you'd like to share with the entire class?"

Bear kept right on talking.

Mr. Spencer whacked the blackboard with his pointer. "Quiet!" he ordered.

Bear stopped talking, then leaned back at his desk.

"You don't have to get all bent out of shape about it!" he said.

"I expect you to pay attention when you're in my class," the teacher replied. His Adam's apple bobbed up and down, and his face, which was normally white and pasty, began to turn red.

Those were definitely danger signs.

But instead of backing off, Bear just shrugged. "I've got more important things to think about than your class," he said.

The entire room gasped. No one talked to Mr. Spencer like that. Ever. Especially Bear. The kid didn't have a mean bone in his entire endoskeleton. Granted, he wasn't the smartest kid in school. He worked really hard just to get D's. But he was one of the nicest . . . or at least he had been.

Mr. Spencer's Adam's apple continued bouncing up and down like a basketball, as his face went past red all the way to purple. He whacked his pointer against the blackboard so hard it splintered into pieces. The kids ducked as wooden projectiles flew over their heads.

But not Bear. He didn't move a muscle.

"My goodness, what's going on in here?" The perky new assistant principal, Miss Perrucci, bounced into the room. She had just happened to be passing by when Mr. Spencer lost his temper.

"I'm sorry, Miss Perrucci," Mr. Spencer said. "But this young man says he has better things to do than pay attention in my class."

"Well, now, I'm sure he didn't mean it that way, did you, honey?" She turned toward Bear and gave him a wink. "Come on, now. Tell Mr. Spencer you're sorry."

"Not on your life," Bear growled. "He's a jerk. And this place stinks!"

For a moment it looked like Mr. Spencer might explode. Finally he waved what was left of his pointer at the door. When he spoke, his voice quivered with rage. "Then maybe you should leave . . ." he ordered, "since your grades indicate it's impossible for you to learn anything anyway."

Now it was Bear's face that turned red. He rose from his seat and threw his pencil down to the floor. He stood there, just glaring at his teacher. Finally he spoke. "How dare you speak to the Phangmaster that way!" he shouted.

"The Phang-whatzit?" his teacher asked.

"I demand an apology!" Bear yelled. "If I fail to get one, you will be severely punished!"

Mr. Spencer stood there, his mouth hanging open, not having the slightest clue as to how he should respond. But not Bear. The kid spun on his heels and stalked toward the classroom door. When he arrived, he turned back to Mr. Spencer. "You'll pay for this," he sneered. "Both you and Miss Perrucci. You're both going to pay."

Mr. Spencer started toward him. "I'll teach you to address your elders in such a manner. Now, you just—"

"WHOAAAA!"

Suddenly he stepped on Bear's pencil. His feet shot out from under him, and for a second he looked like Superman trying to fly.

Unfortunately, his landing was nothing like Superman's.

KER-THWACK!

He lay sprawled out, face up on the floor, without moving.

"Eeeagh!" Miss Perrucci screamed.

"Is he dead?" a student asked.

Mr. Spencer groaned and slowly moved his head. Miss Perrucci hurried to his side and helped him sit up. His glasses were still perched on his nose, but there was no way he could see through their shattered lenses.

"Somebody call a doctor," Miss Perrucci shouted. "Call a doctor!"

"No, no," Mr. Spencer shook his head. "I don't need a doctor. I'm all right."

"Are you sure?"

"Yes, I just need to get up." He rose shakily to his feet. Now all eyes were glued to the assistant principal.

"Why are you all looking at me like that?" she asked.

It was Bear who gave the answer. "You saw what happened when I put the curse on him, didn't you?"

Miss Perrucci just stared.

"Now they're wondering what's going to happen to you."

Miss Perrucci glanced around the room at the students. "Why, that's just . . . that's ridiculous. Surely you don't think Mr. Spencer fell because of something this young man said, do you?"

Nobody answered.

"Well, do you?"

Repeat in the no-answer department.

Finally she shook her head. "Well, that is just so silly. The man stepped on a pencil, that's all. He just—"

KA-BOOM!

Suddenly an explosion shook the windows. Students screamed, and some dove under their desks in terror.

4

BEAR-ly Hanging on to Reality

"Is everybody all right?" Miss Perrucci shouted as she raced to the windows to have a look.

Her question was greeted with a mumbled chorus of yeses and I'm okays.

"It was just that car out there backfiring," she said, pointing through the window. Then, turning back to the class, she continued. "I think we've all let our imaginations run away with us a bit. In any case, I can assure you that neither Mr. Spencer nor I will be intimidated by—"

RRRRRING!

The bell to end class sounded, and immediately students closed their books, leaped from their desks, and headed for the door. Miss Perrucci wanted to continue her speech, but she knew it wouldn't do any good. No one was paying her any attention. That was too bad. Because it would be the last time any of them would see or hear from her in many, many days. . . .

MONDAY, 18:13 PDST

Sean sighed as he set the binoculars on the sidewalk in front of him. "We might as well give up," he said. "Doesn't look like Bear's going anywhere tonight."

"How about letting me have a look?" Melissa asked as she finished eating a banana, then carefully placed the peel into a plastic bag before carefully placing it into her backpack. (You might call Melissa a neat freak. Sean does.)

"Be my guest." Sean handed the binoculars to his sister and sat down on his skateboard. The two of them were keeping an eye on Bear's house from behind a clump of bushes just across the street. Melissa raised the binoculars to her eyes.

Bear's house was quiet. The blinds were drawn, and the only sign of life was a small light burning in an upstairs window.

"I guess you're right," Melissa sighed. "If he was going out, he would have already . . . uh-oh!"

"Uh-oh . . . what?" asked her brother.

"Bear just walked out the front door."

"He did?" Suddenly Sean was on his feet. "What's he doing now?"

"He's getting his bike out of the garage."

"Okay, let's go," Sean said, "but remember what I told you. Stay far enough behind—"

"I know, I know." Melissa rolled her eyes. "So that he doesn't know we're following him." Then, pointing to Sean's skateboard, she added, "Which ought to be easy for you on that thing."

"And just what do you mean by that?" Sean asked indignantly.

"I mean, it's so old that you'll be lucky if you can stay within sight of him. While I, on the other hand . . ." She patted her bright, shiny scooter, which lay on the ground beside her.

"This skateboard can beat that stupid scooter any day of the week," Sean shot back.

"Sure, right, uh-huh." Melissa pretended to yawn.

Sean grabbed the binoculars from her and watched Bear climb onto his bicycle and begin riding away. "I'll prove that to you later," he said, "but in the meantime, we're letting Bear get away. Come on, let's go!"

MONDAY, 18:39 PDST

Miss Perrucci, the assistant principal, checked her rearview mirror once, twice, three times . . . then slowly maneuvered her Ford Escort out onto Highway 47. She was proud of the fact that she was such a careful driver. In fifteen years of driving, she'd never even come close to getting a ticket.

Her best friend, Janice, sat in the passenger seat. They were on their way to a teacher's conference in Hurleyville. Janice was growing more and more frustrated trying to find a decent radio station to listen to. She kept twisting the dial from one station to the next.

"For the deodorant that keeps you smelling fresh as a daisy all day long—"

skzzzzzz

". . . try one of our fresh tuna fish sandwiches. And why not top it off with a big glass of—"

skzzzzzz

". . . Shaker State Motor Oil. With Shaker State, you can be sure—"

skzzzzzz

50

". . . your teeth will be their whitest white, and your breath will—"

skzzzzz

". . . stop roaches dead in their tracks. Plus it will kill flies, ants, fleas, termites, and—"

skzzzzz

". . . all the people you love."

Finally, in frustration, Janice clicked off the radio and leaned back in her seat. "Nothing but commercials," she complained. Then, turning to Miss Perrucci, she said, "So, tell me some more about that student who threatened you."

"There's not much more to tell," Miss Perrucci said. "I feel sorry for him, really." She checked her rearview mirror and prepared to pass the big rig in front of her. Carefully she turned the steering wheel to the left, and her car moved into the passing lane. When she was safely past the truck, she turned the wheel back to the right. Or at least she tried to. But instead of turning, the car just kept moving to the left.

"What in the world?"

She grabbed the steering wheel tighter and twisted hard to the right.

But the car didn't respond.

She tried again, until . . .

THWACK!

. . . the entire steering wheel came off in her hands.

"Uh-oh . . ."

"What's going on?" cried Janice.

But Miss Perrucci had no time to respond. Suddenly the car was off the road and . . .

WHACK! WHACK! WHACK! WHACK!

. . . plowing through the bushes in the center divider.

"The brake!" Janice shouted. "Hit the brake!"

Miss Perrucci stomped on the pedal. It went all the way to the floor, but nothing happened.

"It must be that curse!" Janice screamed. "He cursed you and we're going to die!"

But before Miss Perrucci could answer . . .

KA-POW!

. . . the front tire hit a rock, sending the car sharply to the right and back across the highway, directly in front of a . . .

HONK! HONK!

. . . eighteen-wheeler big rig. The truck driver slammed on his brakes, and his vehicle slid sideways down the highway, spilling its cargo of nails.

POW! POW! POW!

The sound of exploding tires filled the air as half-a-dozen cars skidded to a stop. Fortunately, Miss Perrucci's blue Escort was not one of them. Unfortunately . . .

KER-WHAM!

. . . it tore through the wooden guardrail on the side of the road and disappeared into the woods. Both women covered their eyes and screamed.

Sean and Melissa had followed Bear to a run-down building on the outskirts of town. There, as the young detectives watched from a safe distance, Bear climbed off his bike. Next, he looked around to see if anybody was looking.

For a moment, Melissa's heart leaped into her throat. It seemed as if he were looking straight at her. But then he turned and walked his bike to a large tree where it would be hidden from view. A moment later, he disappeared down the outside stairs leading to the building's basement.

"The Midvale Community Theater?" Melissa asked. "Why did he come here?"

Sean shrugged. "I have no idea. But there's only one way to find out." Without a word he headed toward the stairs that led to the basement. Reluctantly, Melissa followed. But when they arrived the door was locked.

"What do we do?" Melissa whispered. "Knock and see if someone lets us in?"

Sean shook his head. "No way. But we've got to find out what's going on down there." He spotted an empty soda can lying on the ground. Scooping it up, he wiped off the dirt and gunk and placed it against the door.

Melissa watched in confusion as he leaned forward, placed his ear on the other end, and strained to hear what was going on inside.

"What are you doing?" she whispered.

"I saw this in a movie once," he explained.

"Can you hear anything?"

"Nah." Then, offering the can to her, he said, "Why don't you try it?"

"Me? Put my ear against that filthy thing? I don't think so."

"Come on," he pleaded. "Your hearing's better than mine."

After a moment, Melissa sighed, "Oh, all right." She leaned forward, careful not to let her clean hair touch the can. (I told you she was a neat freak.)

Finally she placed her ear on the can and listened. And then, believe it or not . . .

It worked!

She was amazed. She could actually hear voices. They weren't clear, but maybe if she listened just a little bit closer. She closed her eyes tight and pushed harder against the can.

"Don't worry about that stupid teacher," someone was saying. "He'll get what's coming to him."

"Yeah," another voice laughed, "just like we took care of that assistant principal."

"You mean, because I have the power?" asked another voice—one that sounded an awful lot like Bear.

"Yeah, right. Sure, sure, 'cause you have the power," the first voice said.

"Can you hear anything?" Sean asked. But instead of waiting for an answer, he grabbed for the can, causing Melissa to lose her balance, fall forward, and . . .

BANG! "OW!"

. . . bump her head on the door . . . hard.

"Who's there?" someone shouted from inside.

"Somebody's spying on us!" another yelled so loud

that even Sean could hear him.

"Nice work, sis," Sean cried. "Let's get out of here!" Without another word he turned and sprinted up the steps.

5

Mrs. Tubbs,
What a Card

Sean raced up the stairs and kept running until he reached his skateboard. It was only then that he noticed he was racing alone. Melissa was nowhere to be seen.

"Misty!" he called. "Misty, where are you?"

"I'm coming! I'm coming!"

She appeared from the outside stairs, running as fast as she could. And to Sean's surprise, nobody was chasing her.

"Let's go!" she shouted as she arrived and hopped onto her scooter. "They'll be here any second!"

"But . . ." Sean looked back toward the theater building.

He could hear angry voices: "Ooof!" "Ouch!"

"Outta my way!" But nobody was coming after them.

"I'll explain later!" Melissa said. "Let's go!"

Sean didn't have to be told twice. Soon both were racing for their lives down the street.

Meanwhile, back at the theater, Bear's friends kept trying to scramble up the outside steps. But "try" was all they seemed to do. Because no matter how they worked at it, they just kept falling and slipping and sliding until they were one giant pile at the bottom of the stairs.

"What's going on?" the tall redheaded leader demanded as he arrived at the door and tried to crawl over them. "What are you—WOAAA!" And that was all he said before he, too, joined the crowd at the bottom of the steps.

Sean and Melissa raced through the front door and into their house.

"Now, (*huff-puff*) tell me, (*puff-huff*) what were you doing back there?" Sean demanded.

Melissa bent over, trying to catch her breath. "You

know how Dad's been telling us to eat more fruits and vegetables?"

"Yeah . . . like that banana you were eating back at Bear's?"

"Exactly. Well, I brought along a couple extra for you. But since you weren't too interested, I kinda left them behind for our friends."

"You what?"

"I smashed them all over the steps on my way up so they would slip on them."

Sean looked at her a moment, then broke out laughing. "Way to go, sis!" They exchanged high fives. "Talk about giving them 'the slip.'"

Melissa joined in the laughter. "There's just one thing that's bothering me," she said.

"What's that?"

"I'm not sure why we took off running."

"Uh, because they would, like, majorly hurt us," Sean suggested.

"Not if we told them we came to join the group."

"What?" Sean raised his hands. "No way!"

"Why not?"

"I'd want to know a lot more about them before we did anything like that," he said.

"But how?"

"I don't know." Sean paused to think. "The only

other connection we have is that sorcerer book thing and those cards, right?"

"Right," Melissa agreed.

"Then maybe we should go to the Toy Emporium and see what we can find out."

Miss Perrucci and her friend Janice sat in the car with their hands still across their faces. Everything was deathly quiet.

Janice was the first to speak. "Are we. . . ?"

"Are we what?" Miss Perrucci asked.

"Are we, you know . . . dead?"

"I don't think so." Miss Perrucci took her hands from her face and looked around. "We're still in my car."

Janice opened her eyes. "But where is your car?"

Miss Perrucci reached for her window and rolled it down. "We seem to be stuck in mud," she said. "The soft landing probably saved our—"

Bloop . . . bloop . . .

She stopped at the gurgling sound as the car settled deeper into the mud.

Blip . . . bloop . . .

The two women looked at each other, their eyes widening in fear. Then, in perfect unison, they both screamed: "WE'RE SINKING!"

MONDAY, 19:40 PDST

"Good grief! Look at this crowd!" Melissa exclaimed.

Sean nodded. "We'll never be able to get inside."

And he was right. Hundreds of kids and their parents had invaded the Midvale Toy Emporium. Apparently, Cecil What's-His-Name and his Phangdoodle cards had become an overnight sensation. A flashing green light stood on a tall pole to draw attention to the display, but it really wasn't necessary. Shoppers jam-packed the doors leading into the store, pushing and elbowing one another, trying to get to the cards first.

"Look!" Melissa pointed toward a heavy woman not far in front of them. "It's Mrs. Tubbs!"

"What's she doing here?" Sean asked.

"You know how snoopy she is," Melissa said. "She probably just wants to know what's going on."

Suddenly Sean snapped his fingers. "I've got an idea."

"What?"

"Come on, follow me."

With a little squiggling, squirming, and squishing, Sean and Melissa finally managed to squeeze in behind Mrs. Tubbs.

"What are we doing?" Melissa asked.

"If we stay right behind her, we'll be inside the store in no time," Sean whispered. "It's like a football play. You've got to stay behind your blocker."

When Sean was right, he was right. Mrs. Tubbs pushed and shoved her way through the crowd, with the two right behind her. And within a few short minutes all three were standing directly in front of the Cecil Shoemaker display—which wasn't exactly the safest place in the world to be.

"I was here first!" a woman shouted.

"No, you weren't!" a kid shouted back. "I was!"

"Ouch!" Suddenly Melissa took an elbow to the ribs.

"Hey!" Sean stumbled as someone pushed from behind. He turned around and looked into the face of a tall redheaded kid.

"What did you do that for?" Sean asked.

"Because you're in my way!" the kid shouted. "Now, move it!" He forced his way around Sean and began shoving Phangdoodle merchandise into a giant shopping bag.

"Hey!" Mrs. Tubbs shouted. "Leave some for the rest of us!" She grabbed the kid's shopping bag and pulled.

"Stop it, lady!" the redheaded kid cried.

But Mrs. Tubbs pulled even harder, until . . .

RRRIIIIP!

. . . the bag split open. The kid's stash of Phangdoodle goodies spilled onto the floor, and a dozen people scrambled for them.

"Stop it!" he shouted. "They're mine! They're mine!"

But nobody paid attention.

It was an unbelievable scene. Pushing! Shoving! Clawing! Kicking! Worse than Christmas shopping at the mall. (Well, maybe not that bad, but you get the picture.)

And Mrs. Tubbs was doing most of it.

"Mrs. Tubbs!" Melissa shouted over the noise. "What do you want with all this stuff?"

For the briefest moment, Mrs. Tubbs stopped fighting. It was as if she'd never thought about it before. Then she came to and shouted back, "Everybody else wants it, so it *must* be valuable!" And with that she went right back to her pushing and shoving.

Unfortunately, Sean stood right in front of a pack of Phangdoodle cards that she had her eyes on. "Give me those!" She pushed hard, sending him sprawling backward. Trying to keep his balance, he grabbed the pole with the flashing green light.

Big mistake. It was a lot weaker than it looked.

KEE-RASHH!

The green light went falling to the floor as Sean . . .

KER-WHUMP!

. . . landed right on top of it.

And when he did, his digital watch smashed through the big green light bulb.

The lamp popped and hissed. Sparks flew. And suddenly a greenish electrical current began flowing back and forth between the green light and Sean's watch.

Sean looked at it, his eyes widening. "It's going to explode!" he shouted. But everybody was too busy fighting to hear.

Melissa reached down to him. "Here! Grab my hand."

He did. As soon as he was back on his feet, he looked at his watch. Now the digital display was flashing backward. It was impossible to read the numbers as they rushed past, gaining speed. And then, when they finally read 0000:00, the numbers stopped and there was a loud

KA-BOOSH!

Instantly Jeremiah was in the room.

Not in Sean's watch . . . not in Melissa's computer game . . . not even in the monitors for the store's security system. No, Jeremiah was right there in flesh and blood—er, electricity and voltage; a green, glowing creature who looked like he must have escaped from some alien-invader, science-fiction movie!

"Oh boy!" Jeremiah cried. "Phangdoodle cards!"

"Jeremiah!" Melissa half whispered, half shouted. "They'll see you!"

"So what?" he croaked and squeaked at the same time. "They're too busy fighting to care. Don't make a mountain out of a pig's ear."

"Mole hill," Melissa corrected. At times like this, it really shouldn't matter, but she still hated when Jeremiah butchered the English language.

"Whatever," Jeremiah shouted as he hurried toward the Phangdoodle display. "Don't make a mole hill out of a pig's ear."

"Give me those!" the redheaded kid shouted at Mrs. Tubbs. They were involved in a major tug-of-war over a Phangdoodle card deck. So fierce, in fact, the kid's face had turned as red as his hair.

"Not on your life!" Mrs. Tubbs yanked at the cards with all her might and freed them from the kid, causing him to slip and lose his balance. As he fell to the floor, she quickly slipped the prize into her shopping bag.

"You'll be sorry," he shouted as he staggered to his feet. "I'll get you for this, lady."

"Is that a threat?" Mrs. Tubbs laughed.

"No!" the redheaded kid shouted. "It's not a threat, it's a promise! And I always keep my promises!"

6

Slobs Turns Electric

TUESDAY, 8:30 PDST

KC and Spalding were waiting for Sean and Melissa at the entrance to Midvale Middle School.

"Hey, did you guys hear about Miss Perrucci?" KC asked.

"Hear what?" Sean and Melissa answered at the same time.

Spalding's voice trembled with excitement. "Apparently, she has met with some rather unfortunate calamity!"

"What happened?" Sean asked.

"No one knows for sure," KC answered. "But she ain't here today, and no one knows where she is."

"I have heard she was struck by a meteor falling from the sky," Spalding stated.

"I heard she got some sorta disease," said a passing boy.

"I wonder who's going to be next," said his friend.

"All I know," KC chimed in, "is if Bear tells you to do something, you'd better do it."

The group stepped into the school and walked down the hall.

"Has Bloodhounds, Incorporated, been able to discern any further information regarding Bear's disturbing behavior?" Spalding asked.

"Shh . . ." Suddenly KC poked him in the ribs. "He's right behind us."

They turned and, sure enough, there was Bear. Only now he was surrounded by a group of kids known throughout the school as the losers and troublemakers. One of them was the tall redheaded kid Sean and Melissa had seen at the toy store.

"Hey, Bear," KC said, trying to sound friendly. "What's up?"

"Nothin'."

"Did you hear about Miss Perrucci?" Sean asked.

Bear sighed and slowly nodded his head. "She should have apologized to me."

"That's right, she shoulda listened!" the redheaded kid said as he pulled a can of Silly String from his pocket. "And you'll listen, too, if you know what's good for you!" Suddenly he fired the sticky pink stuff at Sean. Sean managed to duck out of the way, but not

Spalding. He took a full blast of it in the face. Soon it was dangling from his glasses and hanging from his ears.

"Hey, you didn't have to do that," Bear said. "Those guys are my friends."

"It's part of the magic," the kid said as he chuckled and they headed down the hall. "Besides, they're not your friends. Not anymore."

When they were out of earshot, Sean jerked his thumb in their direction and asked KC, "Who is that guy?"

KC shrugged. "His name is Fred. He's sixteen and still in the eighth grade."

"He attended my Spanish class last year. I felt rather sorry for him," Spalding said as he continued wiping Silly String from his hair. "Occasionally some of the other students made sport of him."

"Made *sport*?" Melissa asked.

"Teased him," Spalding replied.

"Yeah, well, I can see why," Sean said. "What a jerk."

"Sean," Melissa warned.

"Well, he is."

TUESDAY, 11:47 PDST

Melissa stood in the cafeteria line trying to make up her mind between two horrible lunches. One looked like burnt shoe leather covered with maple syrup, while the other resembled Slobs' favorite dog food.

"Come on, hon, whatcha want?" the muscular lady behind the counter asked. "I ain't got all day."

Melissa smiled politely. "All I really want are a couple of crackers."

"Suit yourself," the woman said.

She tossed a couple packages of Saltines in Melissa's direction. One of them bounced off her tray and onto the floor. When Melissa stooped down to get it, she spotted Bear out of the corner of her eye. He was all by himself. She guessed that his new friends had the earlier lunch period.

Moments later, after she'd paid for her crackers and milk, Melissa decided to join him. Not so much because she was trying to solve the case, but because she was genuinely concerned for him.

"Hey, Bear!" she said, setting down her tray.

"Hullo," he grunted.

She pulled out a chair and sat. "I, uh, noticed you weren't at youth group Sunday night."

Bear shrugged. "I got better things to do."

She could tell he really didn't want to talk about it, but she plowed ahead anyway. "That's too bad, 'cause I know some of us missed you."

"Yeah, right," Bear snorted.

"We did."

"Tell me another one," he sneered. Then, without giving her a chance to respond, he added, "Besides, I got better things to do than read some dusty old book."

His response surprised her. "You mean the Bible?" she asked.

He said nothing, but continued to eat.

"Bear, the Bible's not some dusty old book. It tells us all about God and shows us how to live our lives."

"Yeah, right," he scorned.

"Bear..."

"Listen," he rose to his feet. "Thanks for the sermon, but I'm pretty busy right now. I gotta go." Before Melissa could answer, he picked up his tray and stalked off, looking for a less crowded place to sit.

TUESDAY, 15:30 PDST

As soon as school was out, Sean and Melissa hurried to Doc's house. They had decided that the only way to find out what was happening to Bear was to join his secret society. But they knew they couldn't go as who they were. They had to wear disguises, and they were hoping Doc would have some suggestions.

Then, of course, there was the matter of Sean getting his digital watch repaired. Since the accident at the toy store, no one had seen Jeremiah, and everyone was starting to worry.

"Can you fix it?" Sean asked as he handed her the watch. Then he signed, *I hate to think Jeremiah is still wandering around out there somewhere.*

No problem, Doc signed. After four or five minutes she snapped the watch together and handed it to Sean. It looked good as new.

"Thanks," Sean said as he slipped it onto his wrist and tapped the screen. At first, there was nothing but static. Then suddenly a high-pitched voice spoke:

"Hey, what happened? Where am I?"

"Jeremiah!" Sean smiled. "You're back!"

Sure enough, there was Jeremiah staring out from inside Sean's digital watch. But the angry look on his face made it clear that he was anything but happy.

"How'd I get stuck back in this dump?" he asked, glancing around. "And where did all my friends go?"

"Friends?" Melissa asked. "What friends?"

"My friends in the Phangdoodle Mystical Society."

"The what?"

"You know, the kids that meet down in the basement of the old theater."

"You got in with them?"

"Oh, sure," Jeremiah said. "We're just like birds of a feather who flock separately."

"Together," Melissa corrected him. "Birds of a feather flock together."

Jeremiah frowned and folded his arms across his chest. His face pulsed from red to a deep, dark blue and then back to red. "I want to be back with my friends!"

"But, Jeremiah," Sean protested, "we're your family."

"Family schmamily," Jeremiah snorted. "My friends care about me. And they don't look down on me because I'm green . . . er, blue . . . er, red . . . er, whatever color I happen to be at the moment."

"But, Jeremiah," Melissa protested, "we don't look down on—"

"And they don't even mind that I'm electronic, either. They accept me just the way I am. Well, they will as soon as I introduce myself." He leaned forward until his nose was pressed against the watch face from inside. "I gotta break outta here. I gotta get back into the real world or I'll miss tonight's meeting."

Sean and Melissa exchanged glances. "And when exactly would that meeting be?" Sean asked.

"Meeting?" Jeremiah looked surprised. "What meeting? I didn't say anything about a meeting."

"Sure you did," Melissa said.

Jeremiah grew more agitated. "I don't know what you're talking about," he said. "I was planning on going golf . . . er, swim . . . er, bowling tonight. Yeah, that's it! Bowling!"

"Bowling?" Sean laughed. "When did you take up bowling?"

"I've always loved bowling," Jeremiah said. "I mean, what did you think I was going to do between 7:00 and 9:00 tonight? Hang out in the basement of some old theater with the Phangdoodle Mystical Society?" He laughed nervously. "Don't be ridiculous."

Meanwhile, Doc had returned to her lab bench to continue working on SuperVac. She had concluded that the problem had to do with four faulty microchips. She'd already replaced three of them. One more and SuperVac should work just fine.

Ever so carefully, she picked up the final microchip

with a pair of tweezers. Everything was going perfectly until . . .

"Ah . . . ah . . ." She felt a sneeze coming on.

She did her best to hold it back but . . .

"AH . . . AH . . ."

It kept building and building until finally,

"AHHHHH-CHOOOO!"

Yes, sir, it was a doozy! When she opened her eyes, she was grateful to see she still held the tweezers in her hand. She would have been a bit more grateful if the microchip had still been between them.

She pushed away from the workbench and began searching the floor. Unfortunately, Slobs found it first. Before she could stop the dog, Slobs gave it a curious sniff and then . . .

GULLLLLP!

. . . swallowed it whole.

Now, maybe it was the acid in Slobs' stomach . . . or maybe it was something in Slobs' slobber . . . or maybe it was simply that there are days when everything that *can* go wrong *will* go wrong. Whatever the reason, as soon as that microchip entered Slobs' stomach . . .

VAROOOOOOOOOM!

. . . the SuperVac roared to life. Not only did it roar to life, but it took off and began chasing Slobs!

"Woof! Woof!" The big dog ran around in circles with the vacuum cleaner right behind her.

"Why is it chasing Slobs?" Melissa cried.

No one was sure.

"Run, Slobs!" Sean cried. "Run!"

And run she did . . .

First, through the kitchen. SuperVac was less than two feet behind her and closing the gap!

Then through the den. Now SuperVac was one foot behind her.

By the time Slobs reached the front door, the vacuum cleaner's suction was pulling the hair on her tail.

"AROO!" Slobs howled as she raced out the door and into the yard.

Melissa, Sean, and Doc ran right behind. And once outside on the sidewalk they spotted . . . (no, it wasn't Mrs. Tubbs this time. Instead, it was . . .)

Herbie!

Herbie, the accident-prone engineer from KRZY, their father's radio station. He was on his way back to the station after going home for a short afternoon nap.

"Look out, Herbie!" Sean and Melissa shouted.

At the last possible moment, Slobs leaped high into

the air—like a kangaroo. The vacuum cleaner sped by underneath her and . . .

"YAAGGHHH!"

. . . headed right toward Herbie.

"Look out!" everybody shouted. But it was too . . .

KER-ASH!

. . . late! Way too late. Both for SuperVac . . . and Herbie.

7

Not-So-Beautiful Dreamer

"Aaagh! Get it off! Get it off!"

The SuperVac was stuck tight to Herbie's rear and would not let go. Sean, Melissa, and Doc raced to him and tried to help. But no matter how hard they pulled, the vacuum cleaner remained attached.

"Maybe if we all pulled at the same time," Sean suggested.

The others agreed.

"One, two, three . . . pull!"

The group pulled until they were red in the face, but it was no use.

"Slobs!" Melissa gasped. "We need help!"

The big dog sat down and cocked her head to one side.

"Go get Dad!" Sean shouted. "He'll know what to do."

Slobs barked twice and took off running, but only for a few feet before she stopped and looked back for approval.

"Go on!" Herbie shouted. "Before it sucks me inside . . . GO!"

"Woof!"

Slobs started running again when, suddenly . . .

WHEEzzzz . . .

. . . the SuperVac gave a dying moan, let go of Herbie, and fell to the ground, lifeless.

"Thank goodness!" Herbie sighed, rubbing his rear with both hands. As he did, Sean whistled for Slobs to come back. But as soon as she approached . . .

VAROOOOM!

. . . the SuperVac roared to life again.

"AUGH!" Herbie cried, clasping his rear and fearing the worst.

But it wasn't after Herbie. It was after Slobs again!

"Slobs, run!" Sean shouted.

The dog took off. "Woof! Woof!" But the SuperVac was right on her tail. Literally! The group tried to keep up, but within seconds, both dog and machine had headed down the street, out of sight.

"Poor Slobs," Melissa panted as she came to a stop. "I hope she gets away."

"What happened?" Sean asked. "Why did the vacuum cleaner start working again when Slobs came back?"

"I don't know," Melissa said. "But it's gotta have something to do with that microchip she swallowed."

"You mean she swallowed a microchip that helps power that device?" Herbie asked.

"That's right. What can we do about it?" Melissa asked.

Herbie thought for a moment, but his answer wasn't exactly brilliant. "You just gotta keep your dog and that machine as far apart as possible."

TUESDAY, 16:03 PDST

Things were deathly quiet at the Midvale Police Department.

Chief Robertson sat in his office, feet on his desk, reading the latest Batman comic book (hey, he's got to learn crime fighting somewhere) when . . .

EEEEEEEE!

. . . the quiet was shattered by squealing brakes right

in front of the police station. A short, fat man with a round face raced into the building and yelled out a single word:

"Monsters!"

Chief Robertson took his feet off his desk. "Monsters?" he asked. "Have you been drinking?"

"No, sir," the man shook his head.

"What kind of monsters?" Chief Robertson asked. "And where?"

"Way out in the swamp past Highway 47," said the red-faced man. "I have no idea what they were. Swamp monsters, I guess."

"Swamp monsters?"

"Yeah, they was all covered with mud and slime. Looked real cold and tired, too, like they'd been lost out there fer a while. Horrible-lookin' things."

"Can you take us back out there?"

The man backed away. "Isn't there some other way?" he cried. "It's too scary."

"I'm sorry, sir," the chief said. "But I'll need your help."

Reluctantly, the man started to nod. (Either that or he was shaking so hard it looked like a nod.) Either way, the chief took it as a yes.

TUESDAY, 18:42 PDST

"You sure Bear won't recognize me?" Sean asked.

"Not a chance," Melissa replied. "Your disguise is perfect. How about me?"

"Even I wouldn't know you," Sean said. "Doc did a great job on these disguises."

Melissa nodded. The two were about to visit the meeting of the Phangdoodle Mystical Society, and she didn't want anyone to recognize them. She didn't have to worry. The disguises were perfect. She wore a thick black wig that hung almost to her waist. Dark sunglasses hid her eyes, and at least two pounds of eyeshadow, mascara, lipstick, and other assorted makeup covered her face.

Sean looked even better. His beard gave him the appearance of an Amish farmer. He had wanted to wear a long dark robe to make everyone think he was some sort of mysterious intellectual. Unfortunately, the only thing Doc had was a pink robe with a furry white collar. It didn't look all that mysterious and was anything but intellectual, but it was all they had.

Sean glanced at his watch. "Come on," he said, lifting the robe above his knees so he could walk. "We've got to get a move on."

TUESDAY, 18:54 PDST

When Sean and Melissa reached the abandoned theater, they wondered if the meeting had been called off. There was no sign of life. The place was as cold and deserted as a graveyard.

"What do you think?" Melissa asked.

"I don't know. Did we get the time wrong?"

Suddenly someone stepped out of the shadows. "You guys looking for something?"

It was too dark to see his face, but his voice was very familiar.

"Yes, vee are," Sean said in a thick, not-so-great German accent. "Vee heard zere vas going to be a meeting here tonight."

The stranger moved closer just as the lights from a passing car hit his face. It was Bear!

"I haven't seen you two around here before," Bear said. "Are you new in town?"

"Oh gracious, no. I'm sure y'all seen us before," Melissa answered. (Her southern accent was almost as bad as Sean's German one.) "Y'all probably just don't remember."

Bear no longer saw Sean. Suddenly his eyes were for Melissa, and Melissa alone.

"Oh, I'm sure you're wrong," he said. "Believe me,

I'd remember if I'd seen someone as beautiful as you before."

Melissa turned away, afraid that she was either going to burst out laughing or throw up on Bear's shoes. Instead, she heard herself say, "Why, I'd be surprised if anyone would remember little ol' me. Especially a big, strong, handsome man like yourself."

Bear sucked in his stomach and stood up as tall as he possibly could. Then, doing his best to sound official, he continued. "Well, now, about this meeting. Can you tell me a little bit more—"

"Sorry," Sean interrupted. "Vee really can't talk about itz."

"Besides," Melissa drawled, "it's clear we've made ourselves an itty-bitty little mistake. There's no meeting here, so we all will just be headin' on back—"

Suddenly a voice boomed behind them, "Do they seem worthy?"

"Yes," Bear turned and answered. "They seem very worthy."

Sean and Melissa turned and saw that the other person was . . . some sort of clown? No, that wasn't right. But even in the darkness they could see that this guy was wearing one very bizarre outfit. He had on one of those pointy hats like wizards (and dunces) wear. He also wore a robe that was covered with suns, moons, and stars. And in his right hand he held a can, which was aimed at them.

"Very well," he said. "Then I shall not have to chastise you with the sacred string."

"Sacred string?" Melissa asked. "You mean Silly Str—?"

"Silence!" Bear commanded. "One must never question the High Phang."

As the "High Phang" approached closer, Melissa could suddenly see that it was Fred, the tall redheaded kid. "Let us proceed," he said. "The faithful await."

After exchanging glances, Sean and Melissa followed Fred and Bear down the outside steps to the basement door. Bear knocked twice, paused, then knocked three more times.

Slowly the door creaked open. They entered, stepping onto a small wooden landing. From here they walked down several rickety old steps until they finally arrived at the basement.

The room was jam-packed with kids.

"Hello, brothers and sisters," Bear said. "This is, uh . . ." He gestured toward Melissa.

"Hilda," Melissa said.

"And Arnold," Sean replied.

"Can we trust them?" a voice asked.

"Yes," Bear said. "They are definitely one of us."

Sean and Melissa smiled broadly, trying to show everyone just how normal (or abnormal) they were. They worked their way to a corner of the room, where they could stand quietly and watch what went on the rest of the evening. As they did, Sean leaned toward his sister and whispered, "Do you recognize any of these guys?"

"Yeah," she answered. "I recognize them, but I don't know any of them."

The reason was simple. The group was made up of the outcasts from school—the ones who never got invited to parties, who were anything but popular, and who were always picked last whenever any type of team was chosen.

The crowd grew silent in anticipation as Fred climbed up onto a table. He produced what appeared to be some kind of wand and started waving it over them. "Bless you, my children," he shouted. "I share with you the power of Cecil Shoemaker and the Magic Phangdoodle!"

He closed his eyes and began rocking back and forth. "I summon forth the forces of Phang to smite our enemies," he cried. "Give us power to prevail against those who mock us. Grind their faces into the dirt! Destroy them! Cause their teeth to fall out and their ears to rot away!"

Melissa leaned toward her brother and whispered, "He doesn't seem very nice."

Sean shrugged. "Maybe he had a bad day."

"They will tremble in fear before us," the High Phang shouted even louder. "They will beg for our forgiveness."

And so the evening continued . . . Fred ranting and raving as he cast spells on several of the more popular kids at school, while his followers shouted in agreement and encouragement.

Finally Fred—or the High Phang, if you prefer—held his wand out over the audience and commanded, "Quiet!"

The room grew completely still.

"Now it is time for initiations." He turned toward Sean and Melissa. "We have newcomers here tonight. Arnold and Hilda, come forth to me."

After exchanging nervous looks, Sean and Melissa started forward. Once they arrived and climbed onto the table-stage, Fred draped his arms around them and asked, "Tell us all why you have come here tonight."

Sean was the first to answer. "We all jus' think Cecil Shoemaker is purty durn cool."

Melissa couldn't believe her ears. Suddenly Sean had gone from his German accent to a Texas drawl.

Thankfully, Fred didn't seem to notice. Neither did anyone else.

"And what about you?" Fred turned to Melissa.

"Er . . . ah . . . ditto," was all she could think of to say.

"Wonderful," Fred said. He looked at Bear. "Now the Phangmaster will escort you two out of the building."

"Out of zee building," Sean asked, once again doing his best Arnold Schwarzenegger. "Vvy iz diz?"

"Because we have a small mission we must attend to first," Fred said. Then, waving his wand in the air, he ordered, "Come back in two hours and we will let you know if you have been accepted into the group."

"And then what?" asked Melissa nervously.

"Then you'll go through the initiation." Fred grinned mischievously. He began to chuckle, then laugh. The others joined in. Melissa tried her best to smile. So did Sean. But it's hard to smile when your skin is crawling with goosebumps.

8

The Secret of the Mystical Brotherhood

TUESDAY, 20:30 PDST

"How much more time?" Melissa asked as she sat on the porch of their house with her brother. They'd shed their costumes and makeup inside and were catching some fresh air.

Sean glanced at his watch. "We still have about half an hour," he said.

"Aren't you a little afraid?" she asked.

"Afraid of what?"

"Didn't you see the way they were getting into the ceremony?" Melissa asked. "And that weird laughter? I mean, they were serious."

"Stupid chants and Silly String?" Sean said. "That doesn't sound too serious to me. The worst thing about it is that they're acting like Cecil Shoemaker is some kind of a god or something. I mean, the guy is just a fictional character in a—"

"Help me! Help me!"

They both rose to their feet to see Mrs. Tubbs running down the sidewalk toward them. "Please help me! They stole my cat!"

"Who stole your cat?" Sean asked.

"Devils, that's who!" Mrs. Tubbs broke into tears as she arrived. "Please get my kitty cat back! Please save my sweet bald kitty!"

Melissa put her arm around the old woman. "Don't worry, Mrs. Tubbs, we'll get your cat back. But first tell us what you mean when you say 'devils.'"

"You know," Mrs. Tubbs cried. "Devils! Just like on the Phangdoodle cards."

Sean and Melissa traded looks.

"Phangdoodle cards?" Sean asked. "Mrs. Tubbs, can you start at the beginning?"

Mrs. Tubbs swallowed hard and nodded. "I was looking over my new Phangdoodle cards and watching my favorite soap opera, *The Old and Too Tired to Be Restless*." She took a moment to catch her breath. "I guess I must have fallen asleep or something."

"Then what happened?" Sean asked.

"Then I woke up because they were all laughing at me."

"The devils were laughing?" Melissa asked.

"That's right. There were three of them, maybe four. They were dancing around me and laughing." She was beginning to blubber. "And the tall red one was holding Precious."

Melissa handed her a handkerchief. The woman took it and . . .

SNOORRRK!

. . . blew her nose.

"Thank you, sweetheart," she said, starting to hand it back to her.

"Uh, actually, it belongs to Sean," Melissa answered.

"Just keep it," Sean said quickly. "I've got plenty of 'em."

"Mrs. Tubbs," Melissa asked gently, "did you get a good look at the people who were in your house? Are you sure they were the creatures from the Phangdoodle cards?"

"Well, I didn't have my glasses on," Mrs. Tubbs admitted. "But I know exactly what happened."

"You do?"

"Of course. Those cards came to life, and now Precious is trapped in some kind of Phangdoodle Land." Once again she broke into tears. "Oh, how will I ever get him back?"

Sean exchanged glances with Melissa. "Maybe it would help if we had a look around your house," he suggested.

"Yes, yes," sobbed Mrs. Tubbs. "Do whatever you have to do to save sweet Precious."

Sean was the first to enter through Mrs. Tubbs' front door. It was wide open, just the way she'd left it when she'd run out of the house. Melissa was a few steps behind him.

The television was still on. It cast an eerie, flickering glow across the den. In the light they could see a handful of Phangdoodle cards strewn across the floor.

"I threw 'em at the monsters," Mrs. Tubbs explained.

"And what happened after that?" Melissa asked.

"I don't know," Mrs. Tubbs answered. "I ran and locked myself in the bathroom. When I came out, they were gone."

Sean nodded. Then he and Melissa carefully searched the house. As far as they could tell, everything appeared fairly normal. Well, at least normal by Mrs. Tubbs' standards.

In a back bedroom, Sean whispered to his sister, "You know, she probably just had a bad dream."

"I know," Melissa agreed. "But, then, where's her cat?"

Sean shrugged. "Who knows? He's probably fast asleep somewhere."

After searching inside the house, Sean and Melissa went outside looking for clues. And Melissa was the first to find one. On the ground, underneath one of the back bedroom windows.

"Check it out," she said as she bent down and scooped it up.

"What is it?" Sean asked.

"A Phangdoodle card," she said, handing it to him.

"Correction," he said. "It's *part* of a Phangdoodle card. It's been torn in half. But how do you suppose it got here?"

Melissa pointed at the ground just behind some geraniums. "I suppose it was dropped by whoever made that footprint."

Sean looked at it and nodded. Then he looked up to the window. He began to feel his way around the screen until . . . "Uh-oh."

"What?"

"The screen has been cut," he said.

"Meaning?" Melissa asked.

"Meaning Mrs. Tubbs is telling the truth. Someone broke into her house, all right."

Melissa nodded. "And they probably stole Precious!"

Moments later the two of them were back in Mrs. Tubbs' living room. They were just about to break the bad news to her, when Sean spotted something on the TV.

"Hey," he said, "check it out."

Melissa turned and immediately cried out, "It's Miss Perrucci!"

And she was right. The assistant principal's picture was on the screen, along with the photo of another woman. "What happened to Miss—"

"Shhh!" Sean interrupted. "Listen."

Rafael Ruelas appeared on the screen, his lips flapping about a thousand miles per hour:

"The women are under observation at Midvale Presbyterian Hospital after spending more than twenty-four hours lost in the George Jettison Memorial Swamp, just north of the city," he said. "The two, who are reportedly in good condition, became lost in the swamp after their car went off

Highway 47 yesterday afternoon."

The picture cut to an interview with Police Chief Robertson:

"They were covered with mud, grass, and swamp slime when we found them," Chief Robertson said. "In fact," he chuckled, "we had a report that there were monsters in the swamp. When we got out there we found them standing by the highway, trying to hitch a ride back into town."

"Any idea what caused the accident?" Ruelas asked.

"Miss Perrucci said something about a curse," the chief answered. "But after recovering the car, we're pretty sure sabotage was involved."

"Sabotage?" Ruelas repeated.

"That's right. The brake line was cut with a knife. And there was damage to the steering column."

"In other words?" Ruelas thrust his microphone into the chief's face.

"In other words, someone apparently had it in for these two," the chief answered. "They're very lucky to be alive."

Sean and Melissa stood in silence a long moment. Finally Sean was the first to speak. "Well, what do you know? Looks to me like these Phangdoodlers don't have supernatural power after all. They're just working behind the scenes to make sure their curses come true."

Melissa nodded. "I guess we'd better go to the police and tell them we know who cut the brake line on Miss Perrucci's car."

"Not just yet."

"Sean . . ."

"Hey, we're this close to getting inside the group. Once we're on the inside we'll find out everything these wing-nut guys are up to."

"I don't know, Sean . . ."

He glanced at his watch. "Besides, it's time." Turning to Mrs. Tubbs he said. "Listen, Misty and I have to go to a meeting right now. But I promise, as soon as we get out, we'll start looking for Precious."

"But—" Mrs. Tubbs gave a loud sniff.

"I promise," Sean repeated, "we'll find Precious." Then turning to Melissa, he asked, "Are you ready?"

Melissa hesitated.

"Misty?"

Finally, with a reluctant sigh (and a little shiver), she gave a nod. They started off. But even as they headed down the porch steps, she couldn't resist reciting her favorite quote, "But if we die, you're going to live to regret it."

9

It's a Good Thing Cats Have Nine Lives

TUESDAY, 20:48 PDST

Back at home they quickly changed into their costumes.

"Let's go!" Sean called from the bottom of the stairs. "We're going to be late. Misty? MISTY?!" He tried his best to be commanding (though it's kind of hard to be commanding in a fake mustache, beard, and a pink robe with a white fur collar).

At last Melissa emerged at the top of the stairs in her black wig and sunglasses. Sean couldn't be certain, but it looked like she was wearing even more makeup than the last time. He gave a quiet whistle.

"What?" Melissa demanded.

"If Bear had a crush on you before, he'll definitely be falling in love now."

"Ho-ho," Melissa said, "very funny."

"Well, at least you know you can always have a date for the spring prom," he teased.

Melissa did her best to ignore him as she tromped down the stairs in her high heels. "I still don't feel good about this," she said. "I think we should just go to the police instead."

"Relax," Sean said. "The police will never be able to learn what we can if we go undercover. As members of the group we'll be able to expose everything they're doing."

"I don't know," Melissa said as she arrived at the bottom of the stairs and they stepped out the door. "This is getting pretty dangerous. And what about Mrs. Tubbs' cat and that Phangdoodle card on the ground? Do you think there's a connection?"

"Got me," Sean said as they closed the door and headed down the porch steps. "But we'll find out soon enough."

They'd barely reached the sidewalk when, "Woof! Woof!" Slobs began barking from the side gate.

Suddenly Melissa's face brightened. "Can Slobs come with us?" She turned and rushed over to join the dog. She reached through the gate and gave her a good pat. "You know, just in case there's trouble?"

"Don't be ridiculous," Sean scoffed, "they'd recognize her immediately."

Melissa let out a heavy sigh. "I suppose you're right." Then, turning to Slobs, she said, "Sorry, girl. Guess you'll just have to sit this one out."

Slobs gave her best pathetic whine, but it did no good.

"Sorry," Melissa repeated, "we'll be back soon. Be good." With that, she turned to join her brother. But for the briefest second her long wig got tangled in the gate latch.

"Come on!" Sean urged impatiently.

"I'm coming, I'm coming," she said as she tugged once, twice, then finally freed the wig from the latch. Little did she realize that in all the tugging and pulling she had accidentally lifted the latch. She didn't know it, and neither did Slobs. . . .

At least for the moment.

Sean and Melissa headed down the street. As they passed Doc's house, they saw the light on in her upstairs laboratory. "Looks like Doc is working late again," Sean said.

"Probably on that SuperVac," Melissa said.

"Probably," Sean agreed.

And they were right. At that very moment, Doc was bent over her lab table, carefully installing another power pack into SuperVac. Slobs had given it quite a run for its money the other day, and Doc had decided to increase its power by a few thousand percent.

There had been no more incidents with the dog, which was a good thing. Everyone figured as long as they stayed far enough apart, SuperVac would leave the animal alone.

At least that's what they figured. . . .

TUESDAY, 20: 54 PDST

At last, the moment had arrived. Sean and Melissa—or rather, Arnold and Hilda—knocked on the basement door, were ushered inside the theater, and were now about to be voted into the Phangdoodle Mystical Society.

Fred stood before them in his High Phang getup and pointed his "magic" wand in Sean and Melissa's direction. "Arise," he commanded.

Brother and sister threw glances to each other, then obeyed. They rose from their chairs.

Fred continued. "Congratulations. The Phang has judged you worthy."

Both Sean and Melissa felt a wave of uneasiness wash over them.

"Now there is only one thing you must do to prove your allegiance." Fred turned to another kid, who stood beside him on the table. "Is the sacrifice ready?"

The boy nodded and clapped his hands. Another kid, this time a girl, came forward. She carried a cage with a strange-looking and frightened animal in it.

What is that? Melissa wondered. But only for a moment. Because almost immediately, she realized it was . . . *Precious*!

"Bring the sacred sword," Fred commanded. Then he pointed his wand at Sean and Melissa. "Come forward," he ordered. "You must prove yourselves worthy of our trust by offering this animal upon our altar."

"But that's—that's somebody's pet," Melissa said.

"Yes," Fred agreed, "and they have done me a grave injustice. And now they must suffer the consequences."

"You want us to kill somebody's pet?" Sean asked. "That's crazy. No, that's not crazy, that's just plain sick. No, that's worst than sick, that's—"

"Uh, Sean," Melissa whispered, "I think they get the picture."

Sean turned to the group. The look on their faces said they got the picture, all right. And they weren't too thrilled with what they saw. Or with what they heard. Because, unfortunately, Sean wasn't quite finished. "And we know all about what you did to Miss Perrucci's car. How you—"

"Uh, Sean," Melissa warned.

"—cut her brakes. And how you broke into Mrs. Tubbs' house to steal her cat, and—"

"Whoa, Sean."

"—how you're all a bunch of losers trying to fit in through that stupid book and those wing-nut cards!"

At last he was finished. Pleased that he'd gotten it all off of his chest, Sean looked at the group. If they were unhappy before, they were really steamed now. In fact, many were trading angry looks with one another and starting to rise to their feet. Things were not looking good. Not good at all.

Melissa tried her best to smooth things over . . . or at least try to get out of there alive. "Uh, what my brother here is trying to say—"

"Arnold's your brother?" someone interrupted. "I thought he was from Germany or someplace."

The group began mumbling among themselves.

More were rising. Some started to approach the stage.

Melissa cleared her throat. "Er, I mean, *friend*, what my *friend* Arnold is trying to say."

"Hey, what happened to your accent?" another demanded. The group grumbled even louder as more of them moved toward the stage.

"Uh, laryngitis?" Melissa offered halfheartedly. "When you've got laryngitis, your accent is the first thing to go."

But they weren't buying it—not for a moment. They continued to close in.

"Exkuz mee, Hilda." It was Sean. "But I zink I hav un idea."

"Yeah, what's that?" Melissa whispered, slowly inching away from the approaching group.

"I share it only iv you are oopen to suggestions."

"I'm open, I'm open," Melissa whispered, continuing to back away. "Tell me, what do we do?"

Sean swallowed hard, took a deep breath, then made his suggestion.

"RUN! RUN FOR OUR LIVES!"

No argument there. The two jumped off the table and headed for the stairs as fast as they could. The group lunged for them, some grabbing their arms, others their clothes. For the most part the two managed to slip through the crowd—well, except for the one kid who grabbed Melissa's hair, only to have the wig come off in his hands.

"Augh!" he screamed, throwing it into the air, where it caught in the blades of the ceiling fan and started spinning around.

"DON'T LET THEM GET AWAY!" Fred shouted.

"MEOWRR!" *HISSS*

Suddenly Precious was also loose and running.

"Who let the cat out?!" Fred yelled.

"It's this stupid cage!" Bear lied. "It just opened on its own!"

"Don't let it get away!"

Some of the kids chased Sean and Melissa as they headed for the stairs, while others tried to grab the cat. Eventually, one of the girls managed to scoop Precious up into her arms, but only for a second before he leaped away. Up and away. High into the air, and . . . right on top of Melissa's head—"OW!"— digging in his claws for all he was worth.

The good news was that with all of the confusion, Sean and Melissa were able to get through the crowd and make it to the stairs. The bad news was that for the briefest moment, Precious seemed to be permanently stuck to Melissa's head. Oh, and there was one other bit of bad news. Fred was right on their tail, using the only weapon he could think of . . . his can of Silly String.

They raced up the stairs. But when they arrived at the door, it was locked.

"Now what?" Melissa cried.

"MEOWWWRRR . . ."

They turned toward Precious. He had leaped off Melissa's head and was waddling up another flight of stairs. "Up there!" Sean shouted.

They darted across the landing and started up the steps. Fortunately, Fred had made the stairs and floor behind them so slippery with the Silly String that he and the rest of the group kept slipping and sliding. That gave Sean and Melissa some lead time. Not much, but some.

When they finally reached the top of the stairs, they threw open the door to the theater. It was musty smelling, with more dust and cobwebs than a bad horror movie. Then there was the matter of the light . . . or lack of it.

"Ouch! I hit my knee!"

"Oaf! So did I!"

After tripping and stumbling a few more times along the way, the two managed to race to the front of the theater, where they ducked down between the seats to catch their breath and hide.

Well, at least that's what they were hoping to do.

"Yoo-hoo! Here we are!"

Sean looked down at his watch. It was Jeremiah!

"We're up here behind these front seats! Come and get us!"

Sean glared. "Jeremiah! What are you doing?"

"They won't hurt you," Jeremiah squawked. "They're my friends. They were just fooling around." He yelled again, "Yoo-hoo! Here we are! Here we—"

But that was all he got out before Sean took off his watch and stuffed it in his pocket so Jeremiah could no longer be heard. "Come on," he ordered Melissa, "we've got to move."

And move they did, farther to the side and more toward the corner . . . just as the back door flew open.

"All right!" Fred shouted. "We know you're in here! So why don't you just give yourselves up and make this easier for all of us."

Sean and Melissa crouched lower until they were flat on their stomachs. Then they began crawling under the seats.

"All right, have it your way," Fred called.

Other kids could be heard entering the theater as the search began.

Fred continued. "Just remember that the harder you make us work, the harder it'll be on you."

The footsteps continued to come closer and closer. And closer some more. . . .

10

Making a Clean Sweep

Meanwhile, back at the lab, Doc had inserted the last of the microchips into SuperVac's power supply. And then, after a little noodling here and a little doodling there, *bingo*! Ol' SuperVac came to life just as pretty as you please. Well, just as pretty as you please for about half a minute. Then suddenly, for no reason that Doc understood, the machine began . . .

VARROOOOMing

. . . louder and louder and, more suddenly still, its wheels began spinning.

Before she could catch it, the thing leaped off the bench, hit the floor, and left a long patch of rubber as it peeled out the door and down the stairs. Doc tore off after it, but she was no match for the added power she'd just installed in it. Before she reached the bottom of the stairs it . . .

K-BAMB!

. . . burst through her front door and out onto the street. Of course Doc followed, but by the time she got outside, it was long gone. She had no idea where it had vanished to. If she could hear, she might have been able to know which direction it was heading. She'd also be able to hear something else . . . the distant . . .

"WOOF! WOOF! WOOF!"

. . . of one very frightened dog being chased.

As all of this was going on, Sean and Melissa were crawling on their bellies under the theater seats. If they could just circle around behind Fred and the gang. If they could just reach that back door without being spotted. If they could just—

Thud

Uh-oh. That's the sound Melissa's head made when it bumped into someone's leg. She froze, but it was too late. Suddenly one very big face dropped into her vision. One very big face that looked a lot like Bear.

"You guys see anything?" Fred shouted from across the room.

Bear and Melissa continued to stare at each other, their faces less than twelve inches apart.

"Nobody on this side," someone shouted.

The two continued to stare. Melissa could see something running through Bear's mind, but she couldn't tell what.

"Nothing here, either," another shouted.

"Bear," Fred called, "what about you?"

Bear opened his mouth but did not answer.

"Bear?"

Finally he rose out of Melissa's sight. And then, after what seemed an eternity, he called back. "Nope, nothin' here, either."

A wave of relief washed over Melissa as she lowered her head and continued crawling under the seats. But only for a moment. Because, suddenly . . .

"Come here, you!" A pair of hands reached down, grabbed her shoulders, and pulled her to her feet. It was one of the kids.

"Sean!" she screamed. "SEAN!"

"Here's the other one!" Suddenly Sean was pulled up from the floor by another kid.

"Well, well, well . . ." Fred said, turning around to face them with an unnerving grin. "Look what we've found."

Melissa tried her best to squirm free. "Let go of

me! Let go!" But the burly kid held her shoulders tight.

Sean faired no better.

"Bring 'em back downstairs!" Fred ordered. "Now!"

TUESDAY, 21:18 PDST

Moments later, Sean and Melissa found themselves down in the basement. They were sitting in chairs, their hands tied behind their backs, looking up into the very angry face of Fred.

"We're going to teach you two that you can't mess with the High Phang," Fred sneered. "Just like we showed that stupid assistant principal."

"So," Sean said, "you admit that you messed with the brakes on her car."

Bear, who was standing nearby, turned to Fred. "You did?" he asked. "But you told me it was the curse that—"

"Oh, come on, Bear, you can't be that stupid," Fred said. "I can promise you this . . . she'll never mess with one of us again, no way. We've definitely given her something to remember us by." Then, turning back to Sean and Melissa, he added, "Just like we'll do to your friends here."

"Wha—?" It took Bear a moment to find his voice. "What are you going to do to them?"

Fred turned back to him, that eerie smile filling his voice. "Not what *I'm* going to do, my dear friend. It's what *you're* going to do."

"M-m-me?" Bear asked.

Fred turned and shouted over his shoulder, "Is the sacred sword ready yet?"

"Just about," one of the members called. She was holding a small dagger over the burner of a hot plate.

"Good, very good." Then, turning back to Bear, Fred continued. "I have been given reason to doubt your allegiance to our great Mystical Society, my friend."

Bear swallowed nervously.

"This is a grave matter, but there is one very easy way to clear it up." Fred glanced over to Sean and Melissa, then back to Bear. "Which will it be?" he asked. "Your friends . . . or your brothers of the Society?"

Bear said nothing but swallowed again, even harder.

"The sword is ready!" the girl called.

"Then bring it forth!" Fred commanded.

As the girl approached with the glowing, hot sword, Fred explained, "You, Bear, will have the great honor of searing each of their foreheads with the hot blade of the sword. It will serve as a brand, a mark of warning to the rest of the school, that we of the Phangdoodle are not to be toyed with."

The group of kids murmured in agreement. They obviously liked what they heard.

As the small dagger approached, Bear took a step backward. "I . . . I can't do that."

"And why not?" Fred asked, taking the dagger from the girl.

"Because they're . . . they're my friends."

"Exactly," Fred grinned. Suddenly he reached out and thrust the handle of the dagger into Bear's hand. "And such fierce and terrible action against your very friends shall make us all the more feared."

Again the group murmured in agreement. One or two called out, "Yeah . . . Do it, Bear. Do it!"

"I . . . I can't!"

"Do it, Bear!" Fred ordered. "Do it or else you, too, will wear the sacred brand!"

"But—" Bear continued backing away, until he bumped into one of the other members. "I . . . I can't. They're . . . they're my—"

"ENOUGH!" Fred shouted. Motioning to the

closest members, he ordered, "Grab him!"

Suddenly four or five pairs of hands wrapped around Bear's arms.

"Let me go!" he shouted. "Let me go!"

Fred continued, shouting above him to be heard, "If he does not have the courage to administer the brand, then he, too, shall wear it!"

Bear struggled. "No, let me go. Let me—"

But he was no match for the large number of kids. Soon they were all dragging him toward Fred, forcing him onto his knees before him. Slowly, menacingly, Fred raised the dagger. It looked like Bear would be the first to be branded, followed by Sean, then Melissa. Now the dagger was just inches from his forehead and coming closer by the second, when suddenly—

"WOOF . . . WOOF!"

The outside door flew open and in ran . . .

"SLOBS!" Sean and Melissa cried in unison. Both were thrilled that she'd come to save them. But they couldn't be more wrong. Slobs hadn't come to save them, she'd come to *be* saved. Because right behind her . . .

VAROOOOM!

. . . was SuperVac!

"What is it?" Fred yelled.

"An army tank!" someone shouted.

"An alien spacecraft!" another cried.

But Slobs didn't care what it was, she just wanted to get away. It was only natural that once she discovered the gate was unlocked, she would follow her masters' scent. But now all she could do was run in circles . . .

"WOOF! WOOF!"

. . . around and around, and around some more, with SuperVac right behind.

All this as Fred stood in the middle, yelling, "Stop! Stop this at once!" But it did no good. Or maybe it did. Because, for whatever reason, after several more minutes of running in circles, Slobs had finally had enough. She came to a shaky stop, wobbled this way and that, and suddenly got a funny look on her face.

"Slobs?" Melissa called. "Girl, what's wrong? You don't look so good."

Melissa was right, in more ways than she knew. Suddenly the dog dropped her head right over Fred's shoes and . . .

UR-RU-RRRRP!

. . . covered them in her latest meal of semi-digested dog food.

"Oh, gross . . ." the group groaned.

"You stupid dog," Fred shouted. "Look what you did all over my shoes!"

But if Fred would have looked a bit closer, he would have seen that it wasn't just dog food on his shoes. There was also one very tiny little microchip! The very one that Slobs had swallowed the other day at Doc's.

Immediately the SuperVac stopped in its tracks.

"What's it doing now?" Fred shouted in alarm.

Then, instantly, the SuperVac forgot about Slobs and started racing straight toward Fred, instead.

Fred tried to turn and run but . . .

THER-WHACK!

. . . it was too late! Doc's vacuum cleaner grabbed hold of Fred's rear and wouldn't let go. "GET IT OFF! GET THIS THING OFF OF ME!"

And then, just when it looked like he was about to become SuperVac's latest meal . . .

KE-RASH!

. . . three Midvale policemen, led by Chief Robertson, burst through the basement door with their guns drawn.

"Nobody move!" the chief shouted.

And nobody did.

Except Fred . . .

He got all white in the face, then fainted and fell to the floor, with SuperVac still sucking at his rear.

"Get those kids untied," Chief Robertson ordered his men.

"How did you know we were here?" Sean asked as they began to untie the ropes.

"Somebody called us," the chief answered.

"But nobody knew we were here," Melissa said.

Chief Robertson shrugged. "It was somebody with a real strange voice. Kinda high and squeaky. Almost like it was electric or something."

Sean and Melissa looked at each other and grinned. Each knew what the other was thinking . . . *Jeremiah*!

"What's going on here, anyway?" the chief asked. "Somebody tell me what happened."

"It's a long story," Sean said, rising to his feet and rubbing the feeling back into his hands. "Got a couple of hours?"

The chief gave him a look and nodded. "I'm all ears."

TUESDAY, 22 : 37 PDST

After carefully explaining to the police everything from the Phangdoodle books to the cards, to the attack on Miss Perrucci's car, to the break-in and theft of Precious, Sean and Melissa were finally able to go home. The chief had called Dad, and he was on his way to pick them up.

But as they sat on the steps waiting, Jeremiah appeared on Sean's watch, glowing a deep shade of blue and hanging his head in sorrow. "I thought they were my friends," he said.

"I'm sorry, Jeremiah," Sean said. "But we're sure glad you called the police."

"Yeah," Melissa agreed. "You saved us, Jeremiah."

"They really pulled the wool over my ears," Jeremiah said.

"Please, Jeremiah," Sean said, "just forget about it."

"I promise, from now on I'll always put my money where my nose is. I won't bite the hand that weeds me. And I—"

"Jeremiah?" Sean asked.

"Yes?"

And then, in perfect unison, both Sean and Melissa repeated, "Forget it!"

FRIDAY, 15:30 PDST

By Friday, Miss Perrucci was well enough to return to work. And as school was letting out, she approached Sean and Melissa outside the front doors. "Hey, you two," she said.

"Miss Perrucci." Melissa grinned. "Are you okay? We heard about your accident."

"I'm fine," the assistant principal said. "And I heard about you catching the kids who sabotaged my car."

"No sweat," Sean said, once again forgetting how to be modest. "It's all part of our agency's work."

Melissa could only roll her eyes.

"I understand it was some sort of club or something," Miss Perrucci said. "And that Bear was part of it."

"Something like that," Melissa said. "But please don't be angry with him. He's just always had a hard time finding kids who like him. And when he finally did—"

"They were the wrong type," Sean explained. "Getting all carried away with sorcery and stuff."

Miss Perrucci nodded. "I've asked one of the

counselors to spend some time with him to see if she can help."

"And Sean and I are going to try to be better friends for him," Melissa added.

Miss Perrucci smiled. "That's good, guys. Real good. Because sometimes it's the loners who need the most care and attention."

"Yeah," Sean said. "They're usually the ones who get caught up in all the weird fads and stuff."

"Uh, not always," Melissa said, trying not to giggle.

"What do you mean?" Sean asked.

She motioned across the street to KC and Spalding. Both were wearing long silver antennae that seemed to be sprouting from their heads.

"Hey, guys!" KC waved to them. "What do you think?" Before Melissa or Sean could reply, she continued. "Aren't they great? They're the latest rage! Right from the new *Marty the Martian* TV show!"

Melissa opened her mouth. She was about to point out how ridiculous they looked, but before she could speak, half a dozen other kids joined them wearing the same outfit. Melissa bit her lip, trying not to laugh.

"Well," Miss Perrucci said, also trying to keep a straight face. "Apparently it's not just the loners who can get caught up in fads."

Now the kids across the street were hopping up and down, getting all their antennae to bounce in sync. If they looked foolish before, they looked downright absurd now.

"I guess you're right," Melissa said.

But Sean barely heard. "Hey," he shouted, "where did you get those?"

"Down at the Midvale Toy Emporium," KC called back.

"Really?" Sean asked.

"Yeah, but you gotta hurry. There are only a few left."

"I hear you!" Sean shouted. "I'm on my way!" He turned and started to run.

"Sean!" Melissa called.

"Don't worry!" he shouted over his shoulder. "I'll get you one, too! It'll be great for the agency's image!"

"Sean!"

But it was too late. Her brother was already gone. Melissa looked after him, slowly shaking her head. Then, glancing back to Miss Perrucci, they both broke out laughing. Because no matter how things change, they always seem to remain the same. Especially when it comes to big brothers. And especially when it comes to Bloodhounds, Incorporated.

By Bill Myers

Children's Series:

Bloodhounds, Inc. — mystery/comedy
McGee and Me! — book and video
The Incredible Worlds of Wally McDoogle — comedy

Teen Series:

Forbidden Doors

Adult Novels:

Blood of Heaven
Threshold
Fire of Heaven
Eli
When the Last Leaf Falls

Nonfiction:

The Dark Side of the Supernatural
Hot Topics, Tough Questions
Faith Encounter
Just Believe It

Picture Books:

Baseball for Breakfast